LITTLE PEAR *and the* RABBITS

LITTLE PEAR

Written and Illustrated by

and the RABBITS

ELEANOR FRANCES LATTIMORE

WILLIAM MORROW & COMPANY, *New York*

To

ELISABETH BEVIER HAMILTON

CONTENTS

LITTLE PEAR *and the* RABBITS

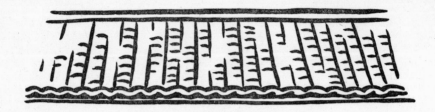

CHAPTER I

LITTLE PEAR OF SHEGU

LITTLE PEAR was a Chinese boy. He lived in Shegu, which was a small, dust-colored village with wide fields all around it. In the wintertime the fields were dust-colored like the village, but in the spring they were green with growing vegetables.

Little Pear's father was a farmer, and he grew fine vegetables: turnips, carrots, cabbages, and beans. Some

13

of the other men in Shegu were farmers too. They shared a mule among them, because mules were expensive. Each farmer had his own tools, though, and his own wheelbarrow for carrying food to the market.

Little Pear wanted to be a farmer when he grew up. In fact, he wanted to be a farmer *now*. But his father said, "You are too little to be a farmer, Little Pear. You must wait until you get bigger."

And his sister Dagu said, "You should go to school first. School is the place for small boys like you."

There was a school for boys in Wuku, three miles from Shegu, and Little Pear had heard some of his friends tell about it. The boys sat at their desks in a row, reading their lessons aloud. They had to do what the teacher said, and they could not go outdoors and play. Little Pear liked to be outdoors, and he loved to play. "I don't want to go to school," he said.

"You don't have to go to school—yet," said his mother, thinking of how far Little Pear would have to travel. Three miles was a very long way for short legs like his. "You must wait until you get bigger."

"And when I am bigger I will be a farmer," said Little Pear.

While Little Pear grew bigger he stayed at home

with his mother and helped his sisters, Dagu and Ergu, take care of the baby, Shing-er. But taking care of a baby was such hard work that Little Pear often thought he needed a change, so he stepped through the gateway that separated his home from the village street. When Shing-er tried to toddle after him, Little Pear shut the gate, for one way to mind a baby was to keep him safely at home.

Everybody in Shegu knew everyone else, and it gave Little Pear a friendly feeling to walk down the street. The candy seller was a friend of his and so was the barber. The candy seller traded candy for pennies, and the barber shaved Little Pear's head—all except for one patch of hair that was allowed to grow and was braided into a small pigtail. It was tied with bright-colored string, sometimes green and sometimes red. Little Pear's mother admired the pigtail, and so did his sisters.

One cold winter day Little Pear started off down the village street. His pigtail was hidden under a cap with fur-lined flaps over the ears, and he wore two coats. The cold could not get through his warm clothes, but it stung his round face and chilled his toes in his cloth-soled shoes.

"Where are you going, Little Pear?" asked his friend Big Head, who had just stepped into the street from the gateway of his home. "Are you coming to play with me?"

Little Pear shook his head. "My mother has sent me to buy wood," he said importantly. It made him feel quite big to be sent on an errand.

"Come back when you have bought the wood," called Big Head, as Little Pear hurried on toward the wood seller's shop.

All through the fall Little Pear and his sisters had raked up dry leaves to kindle the fire that kept their house warm. They had gathered twigs blown from the trees that grew beside the highroad. But twigs and leaves were not enough for the cold winter months, and Little Pear's mother had to buy both charcoal and wood. There was charcoal in the house today, but the wood was all gone. That was why Little Pear had been sent on this errand.

"Candy! Sugar candy! All kinds of candy!" Here came the candy seller with his trayful of candy. But Little Pear could not spare a penny, even for candy. "You must buy twelve pennies' worth of wood, and here are twelve pennies," his mother had said. "Don't stop to play, or you might lose the pennies," advised Dagu. "Hurry, because the house is cold," added Ergu.

"I cannot buy any candy today," said Little Pear

to the candy seller. And he went on his way, though his feet lagged a bit. He could smell the candy, and he could almost taste it in his mouth. Oh, how he wished that the number of pennies in his pocket would grow!

The wood seller's shop was at the end of the village street. It was crowded today, for many people needed to buy wood. The barber was buying wood, and so was the toyshop man. They smiled at Little Pear when he came into the shop. "Here comes your biggest customer," said the barber jokingly, and pushed Little Pear toward the wood seller.

The wood seller leaned over the counter to look at Little Pear. "How much wood do you want? A dollar's worth?" he asked.

Little Pear felt in the pocket that was inside his coat. "No, I want twelve pennies' worth, because I have twelve pennies," he said. He drew out the pennies, one by one, and put them up on the counter. "There are my twelve pennies," he said, when he had come to the last one.

The wood seller peered at the pennies and counted them over twice. "You have made a mistake, Little Pear," he said. "There are only eleven pennies."

"No, there are twelve," said Little Pear. "My mother counted them."

"Count them yourself," said the wood seller.

But Little Pear said, "No. My mother gave me twelve pennies, and they are right there."

The barber laughed, and the toyshop man said,

"Little Pear cannot count to twelve, but if he went to school he would learn very quickly."

"Never mind," said the wood seller. "His mother will buy more wood, so I will let Little Pear have twelve pennies' worth today."

When the wood, tied in a bundle, was handed to Little Pear, he hurried toward home, thinking that of course there had been twelve pennies! Just to be sure, though, he felt in his pocket once more. There was no other penny there, but there was a tiny hole. And when Little Pear was halfway home he saw a copper

penny lying in the street, where it caught the sun's light. Here was the lost penny that had slipped out through the hole! Little Pear picked it up before anyone else could find it. Now, he thought, he had a penny just for himself!

The candy man was still selling candy. Little Pear bought a penny's worth and trudged home happily with his bundle of wood. "Here is the wood—twelve pennies' worth," he said to his mother.

"Thank you, Little Pear," said his mother. "Now we can be warm!"

But Dagu and Ergu looked at their brother, who was munching candy. "Where did you get the candy?" they asked.

"With the other penny," said Little Pear.

His mother was puzzled. "You cannot count," she said, shaking her head.

But whether Little Pear could count or not, the house was warm that day, and he was glad he was big enough to be sent on errands.

CHAPTER II

LITTLE PEAR AND THE KITCHEN GOD

ABOVE the stove in Little Pear's home there hung a beautiful picture. It was a picture of the god who watches over kitchens and sees everything that happens in the house. The kitchen god was kind, so Little Pear's mother said. But to Little Pear and his sisters he looked rather stern.

There he sat, with his wife beside him and his children in a row. They were all dressed in rich, flowing robes, like the kind people wore in China long, long ago. Their colors brightened the plain room and made it look gay. Toward the end of the year, though, the colors began to fade, and smoke from the stove smudged the god and his family.

"When the New Year comes, we shall have a new god in our house," Ergu told Little Pear.

"But there is just one kitchen god," said Little Pear.

"No, there is a new one every year," Ergu insisted. "On the last day of the Old Year, Father will burn this picture; but you must be very good till then. For when the kitchen god goes to heaven, he will report on you. Every time you are naughty, he knows."

"I haven't been naughty today," said Little Pear.

It was not long till the New Year, and Little Pear felt anxious. He wanted the kitchen god to say that he was a good boy. He asked his mother every night if he had been good that day, and he glanced up at the kitchen god as he spoke.

Dagu and Ergu did not worry about what the

kitchen god would say when he traveled up to heaven
and made his report, for they were well-behaved girls.
They helped their mother with the housework, and as
the New Year drew near they were very busy sewing,
making new coats for their little brothers.

Dagu and Ergu liked to take their sewing next door,
where there was a whole family of little girls. They
sat cross-legged on the k'ang in their friends' home
and chattered as they stitched. The k'ang was a big
brick bed with a fireplace in its side, and the glowing
coals kept it warm on even the coldest days.

Little Pear missed his sisters. When he followed

them next door they shooed him home, saying that his mother needed him. When he came back home, his mother told him that he must mind Shing-er, who kept getting in her way while she was cooking dinner.

"I am going to Big Head's house," Little Pear said to his mother. "Shing-er must stay at home, though. He is too little to play with us."

"But Shing-er is your little brother," said his mother. "He needs you to look after him, because you are so big."

"Yes, I am big," said Little Pear. He edged toward the door.

"If you go out, you must take Shing-er," said his mother firmly.

Little Pear looked up at the kitchen god on the wall, and the kitchen god seemed to look straight into his eyes. So Little Pear buttoned up Shing-er's coat and tied on his knitted hood. "Come, Shing-er, we are going to Big Head's house," he said.

Ay-ah, but it was cold outside! A wind whipped down the street, almost knocking the little boys over. Shing-er began to cry. "Cold!" he said.

"The wind is cold, but Big Head's house will be nice and warm," said Little Pear. "Walk faster, Shing-er." But Shing-er would not walk at all. He sat down in the street, and the icy wind blew in his face, making his tears freeze.

Little Pear wanted to see Big Head, but he could not leave Shing-er. He lifted his brother in his arms and carried him back to his mother. "The wind is too cold for Shing-er," he said.

"Never mind," said his mother. "I have finished cooking dinner now, and you can play in the house. Watch Shing-er for a little while longer, and do not touch the stove. I am going to the house next door to call Dagu and Ergu."

"I will call them for you," said Little Pear, wanting to be good.

But his mother said no. She wanted to see the new coats that Dagu and Ergu were making for Little Pear and Shing-er, which were meant to surprise them.

Little Pear was sorry that he had to stay in the house. Shing-er was smiling now, but he smelled the food on the stove and all he would say was, "Eat, eat!"

"Cheep, cheep," said the family pet, a yellow bird that lived in a cage. The bird was hungry too, thought Little Pear.

"We must wait until Mother comes back," he said to Shing-er. For Little Pear must not touch the stove, which was very, very hot. He could touch the bird cage, though, which hung from a hook near the window. Little Pear climbed up on a stool and looked inside the cage. The little dish for birdseed was nearly empty, so Little Pear scrambled down and fetched some more from a jar.

The bird stopped cheeping, and pecked the seeds; but Shing-er could not eat seeds, and he was still hungry. He reached his hands toward the cooking pot on the back of the stove and kept on saying, "Eat, eat!"

The dinner smelled good; it was soup made of cabbages and onions and little bits of meat all cooked together. Little Pear realized that he felt just as hungry as Shing-er. He looked at the stove, which he must not touch, and he looked at the cooking pot. Then he looked at a long-handled spoon, hanging from a nail.

If he scooped just a little soup from the pot with the long-handled spoon, he would not have to touch the stove, Little Pear thought. So he moved the stool over to the stove and lifted down the spoon.

Shing-er's eyes were bright with interest as he watched his brother. "Stand back, Shing-er," said Little Pear. "Do not touch the stove!" He reached across the stove with the long-handled spoon—and just as he was dipping out some soup from the pot, Shing-er came too close and joggled the stool. Out flew the spoon from Little Pear's hand, spattering hot soup! And down fell Little Pear, barely missing the hot stove. "Ay-ah, ay-ah!" cried Little Pear. "Look what you did, Shing-er!" Shing-er began to cry, and the bird began to cheep again— and in through the door walked Little Pear's mother, and Dagu, and Ergu.

"Oh, Little Pear," cried his mother. "Have you hurt yourself?"

"You naughty boy!" said Dagu. "What have you been doing?"

"Hush, Shing-er, hush," said Ergu, picking up Shing-er.

All three stared at Little Pear, and their faces looked so cross that he felt ashamed. "Shing-er was hungry, so I wanted to feed him," he said softly. Then he added, in a louder voice, "I did not touch the stove."

"But look!" cried Ergu, pointing. "Look at our kitchen god!" Soup had spattered on the picture of the kitchen god.

Ergu's eyes were round and so were Dagu's, as they gazed at the picture above the stove. But their mother smiled. "Perhaps the god was hungry too," she said. "Come, children, let us all eat our dinner now."

Little Pear was not quite sure whether he had been naughty or not. But the kitchen god could not have been very cross with him, for the new picture that was put on the wall in the New Year showed a smiling god, not a stern one.

CHAPTER III

NEW COATS FOR THE NEW YEAR

THE New Year in China begins with a lot of fire-crackers, and the fun and feasting last for two whole weeks. Special little cakes are baked, with New Year's greetings on them. These cakes were good-luck cakes, Little Pear's mother told him; and he ate so many that he felt sure he would be very lucky.

"I am going to be lucky in the New Year," he said to his mother.

"You are lucky now, Little Pear," she said. "Look at your fine new coat!"

Little Pear looked at his coat, which was almost too grand to wear. It was made of shiny green cloth, and it was trimmed with braid. Dagu had sewn the seams; Ergu had put on the trimming. Yes, this new coat that his sisters had made was a fine one, he thought.

When Little Pear put on his new coat, his sisters were very proud of him. "You look like an emperor's son," said Ergu, clapping her hands.

"You look very grand," said Dagu. "But don't get

that new coat dirty!" For she thought of all the hours that she and Ergu had spent sewing, and she knew how roughly little boys sometimes played.

But Little Pear had no idea of getting his coat dirty. He wanted to walk down the street and show it off to his friends.

On either side of the front gate of Little Pear's home there were two stone lions with curly manes. They sat like watchdogs guarding the gate and made it look important. Little Pear stepped through the gate very importantly and paused for a moment between the two stone lions.

The street looked new today, for doors had been freshly painted, and roofs had been mended in time for the New Year. The air was filled with delicious smells from holiday feasts, mingled with the exciting smell of exploded firecrackers. Children, all dressed in their new clothes, had come outdoors to play, and Little Pear ran eagerly down the street to join them.

A boy named Tang had a new top. A boy named Yang had a new whistle. Ay-ah! thought Little Pear, forgetting about his coat.

But Big Head had seen him coming, and he noticed the bright coat right away. It was gayer and more dazzling than anyone else's. "That can't be Little Pear," said Big Head, blinking his eyes.

"Oh, yes, that is Little Pear," said his little brother Didi.

Of course Big Head knew perfectly well that Little Pear was Little Pear, though he pretended not to.

"I see a stranger coming down the street," he announced. "Who is it? Is it a boy or a girl?"

"I am a boy!" cried Little Pear. "I am Little Pear!"

"Oh, yes, I see who you are now," replied Big Head. "I didn't know you at first, because of your funny coat."

"My coat is not funny. It is *new*," said Little Pear.

Little Pear felt indignant at Big Head's remarks; but Big Head, though he was teasing him, was really envious. He wished that he had a fine green coat, trimmed with fancy braid.

The coat that Big Head's mother had made him for the New Year was exactly like his old one, only bigger. It was blue, the usual color of everyday clothes in China, and Big Head suddenly felt that it was too ordinary. He would not admit this to Little Pear, though. Instead, he said to him, "I thought at first that you were wearing Ergu's coat. See, my new coat is plain, and *big*. It makes me look like a man. Nobody would ever think that I had on a girl's coat."

Little Pear looked at his friend's coat and felt rather sad. He wished that Dagu and Ergu had made him a plain, big coat. He would not admit that to Big Head, though. He went off down the street to watch Tang spin his top and hear Yang blow his whistle.

"Wait, Little Pear!" called Big Head. "If you don't like your new coat, I will put it on and let you wear mine."

Little Pear turned back joyfully. He was glad to trade coats. When he had put on Big Head's coat he felt just like a man; and Big Head, in the bright green coat, felt like an emperor's son.

It was fun watching a new top spin. It was fun to blow on a New Year's whistle. And Little Pear played with his friends for a long, long time. He played until something inside him told him that he was hungry. Then he hurried homeward, still wearing Big Head's coat.

The lions beside the front gate said nothing to Little Pear, for although their mouths were opened wide, they were made of stone. But when Little Pear's family saw him, they had a great deal to say. "What have you done with your beautiful coat, Little Pear?" asked Dagu.

"Oh, Little Pear, didn't you like it?" asked Ergu.

Little Pear looked from one to the other. "Yes, I liked my coat. But Big Head liked it even better," he said.

"What a naughty boy you are, Little Pear!" said his mother, guessing that he had traded coats with Big Head. "You left home in a fine green coat, fit for an emperor's son, and you come home in a plain blue one, much too big for you."

"It is Big Head's coat," said Little Pear.

"I thought so," said his mother. "Big Head is older than you—and I think he is smarter, too."

Little Pear thought over his mother's words as he went back to Big Head's house; and the more he thought, the more he wanted his own coat back. He was not a man, and this big coat made him feel very small. Ay-ah, he thought, what if Big Head would not trade back?

But Big Head, as it turned out, also wanted his own coat. His father and mother had teased him for wearing a coat too small for him. "You are not Little Pear; you are Big Head," they said. And Big Head liked being Big Head. He traded coats joyfully, and both boys were happy.

There were still some New Year's cakes left when Little Pear came home again, and he ate six of them, because he was so hungry. They were lucky cakes, and he was a very lucky boy, for he had a beautiful new coat to wear through the New Year.

CHAPTER IV

LITTLE PEAR FOLLOWS TRACKS
IN THE SNOW

THERE was ice on the pond beyond the village, and even the river was frozen, but that did not keep Little Pear's father from fishing. He fished through holes cut in the ice, and he used a long, spiked pole. The fish were sleeping in the mud at the bottom of the icy river, and the pole was for spearing them.

Fishing was a cold sport, though. When Little Pear

43

watched his father he felt the ice numbing his feet through his shoes. He could not stand still very long, but had to run and slide before his feet turned into lumps of ice. But Little Pear's father wore special shoes whenever he went fishing: big, clumsy overshoes, fashioned of straw. These shoes were not at all handsome, but they kept his feet from freezing and he could stay out on the ice for hours at a time.

Once Little Pear borrowed the straw shoes, on a day when his father had gone to the village of Wuku. His father took the wheelbarrow, and since it was empty Little Pear had begged to be allowed to ride on it. But his father said, "No, Little Pear. The wheelbarrow is empty now, but it will not be empty when I come back from Wuku. I may be gone one day, or I may be gone two; but when I come home I will bring two pigs to fatten."

Little Pear felt very excited, for he wanted to see those two pigs. He waited and waited for his father one whole day. When he opened his eyes on the next day, he found that the world had changed, for snow had fallen during the night. The house was lit by a still, white light; the courtyard was covered with snow. Little Pear ran to the front gate. There was snow in

the street, too! It was a long time since Little Pear had seen any snow, and he wanted to explore the white world all by himself.

As soon as he had eaten breakfast, Little Pear put on his old coat, which had a quilted lining sewn inside. He put on his winter cap, and then he spied his father's shoes—the straw overshoes that he wore when he went fishing. The snow looked soft as goose feathers and warm as a quilt, but Little Pear knew that it was really cold, like ice. So he asked his mother, "May I wear my father's shoes?"

"Your father's shoes are on his feet," said his mother, laughing.

"His *straw* shoes," said Little Pear.

"Oh, yes," said his mother. "Your father would not mind if you wore his straw shoes."

Dagu and Ergu bundled up Shing-er and took him

out to see the snow, but Little Pear put on the straw shoes and walked off by himself. The snow in the street had already been trodden by people's feet, and the village women were sweeping it away from their doorsteps. But snow lay fresh and smooth and clean over the fields, and it was toward the fields that Little Pear turned. Here nobody had walked before, and he felt

like an explorer. Flop, flop, he walked in the straw overshoes. They were far too big for him, but his mother had tied them tightly around his ankles and they did not fall off.

The sun on the snow was dazzling, and at first Little Pear could not see anything but shining white. As he got used to the brightness, though, he noticed tiny tracks. No person had walked across the fields before Little Pear, but some small bird had walked this way.

Its tracks were just as fine as embroidery stitches.

Little Pear followed the bird tracks until they stopped. He was far from the village now, almost to the highroad. The bird must have flown up in the sky; but Little Pear found other tracks. These new, different tracks looked like the paw marks of a cat.

Little Pear glanced around and saw the distant village and the nearby highroad, with trees along its bank. A brown horse and a blue cart were silhouetted against the sky, but there was no catlike shape cross-ing the snowy field. Cats liked to stay by warm house fires on cold days like this. Little Pear wondered, with a shiver, if the tracks he had found were a fox's. He had never seen a fox, though he had heard stories about them. The foxes he had heard about were usually en-chanted, sometimes taking the form of a man or a woman; but they remained foxes and were not to be trusted. Little Pear did not want to meet a fox.

He almost turned toward home right then. But he was an explorer! Besides, a small dog might have made those tracks, thought Little Pear. Dogs were never enchanted, and he was not afraid of them. On he walked, flop, flop, in his father's overshoes. They were big and clumsy, but his feet kept warm inside of them.

It was fun to explore the countryside on a cold, sunny day and to have the field and the highroad all to himself. Little Pear forgot about following tracks when he climbed the bank to the highroad.

The horse and cart had passed on, and the road led straight ahead between its rows of bare trees, that looked black against the snow.

The highroad led to Wuku, and Little Pear thought

that if he kept walking he might meet his father. It was time that his father came home, bringing the two pigs. Little Pear shaded his eyes from the sun and looked far ahead, but he could not see any wheelbarrow and he could not hear the pigs, which would certainly be squealing.

The road was as bumpy as a washboard under its layer of snow, and Little Pear stumbled in the ruts that cart wheels had made. He slipped and slid in his big shoes. He slid right down the bank! That was fun, thought Little Pear, dusting the snow from his coat. It was fun—but all at once he wanted someone to play with. Back in the village, the other boys would be playing in the snow.

So back toward the village went Little Pear, and no fox crossed his path. But what big tracks were these that he saw, marking the snow? Here were big, wide tracks—so big and so strange that Little Pear felt startled. Nothing but a bear could have made such tracks, which were bigger than a man's footprints and twice as wide! Bears lived in the mountains that lay to the north, and though Little Pear had never seen one, he had heard how big bears were. Ay-ah, ay-ah, he thought, they were more frightening than foxes! Worst of all, the bear tracks led straight to Shegu.

If Little Pear went back to the highroad he would be all alone, and if he went on home he might meet the bear. He paused for a moment, wondering what he should do. Home would be warm, and when he reached home dinner would be ready. Little Pear was hungry, so he started on toward home. After all, if a bear had suddenly come to Shegu, some of the village men would catch it right away.

Little Pear could hardly wait to tell his family about

how he had found the bear tracks in the snow. If they began telling him how the bear was caught, Little Pear would show no surprise! "I saw its tracks," he would say.

He was following them still. But the curious thing was that they led straight to his own house, which was the first one in the village. When he stepped through his own gateway, though, Little Pear saw no more tracks. His mother had swept the courtyard clean.

Little Pear pushed open the front door. "Where is the bear?" he cried.

His mother, Dagu, and Ergu all turned to stare at him. "There are never any bears around here," said his mother.

"But I saw bear tracks," said Little Pear. "And they came right to our house!"

Dagu and Ergu began to laugh, but Little Pear's mother said, "Show me the bear tracks, Little Pear."

Little Pear took her hand, and pulled her out to the gate. There were the tracks, big and clumsy, plain to be seen.

"Look at your shoes," said Little Pear's mother.

He looked at his shoes. The straw overshoes, big and clumsy, exactly fitted the tracks.

"I fooled you," said Little Pear. "There was no bear!"

Little Pear was glad there were no bears tracking through his village, but he looked forward to seeing the pigs his father would bring home. In the meantime, he was hungry, and dinner was ready.

"Let's feed the bear first," said Ergu, looking at Little Pear.

CHAPTER V

LITTLE PEAR TAKES CARE
OF THE PIGS

Dagu sometimes seemed almost as old as her mother. She could cook just as well, she could sew just as well, and she liked keeping house. Ergu, though, was only two years older than Little Pear and she enjoyed playing more than doing housework.

Ergu liked the two young pigs that her father

56

brought home just as much as Little Pear did. She did not agree with her mother and Dagu that pigs smelled bad. Pigs were as pleasant as cats if they were kept clean, she said.

There was no room in the courtyard for two young pigs to grow in, but a neighbor, Mr. Fan, had a pen

that he was willing to rent. The pen was in a yard behind Mr. Fan's house. It was large and roomy, with a roof of mud and straw. There were two troughs in it, one for food and one for water. Mr. Fan rented this fine pen for ten cents a week, but he made it clear that he would not take care of the pigs. "The pen is my business, but not the pigs," he said to Little Pear's father. "You will have to feed and water the pigs yourself."

Little Pear's father said that was quite fair. Of course he would care for his own pigs. He was very busy, though, as he told his family. The snow was melting, spring was coming, and he had to work with the other farmers, getting the fields ready for planting.

"I will feed the pigs," said Ergu eagerly.

"I will fetch the water for them!" cried Little Pear.

Their father smiled, thinking what good children he had. "If you help each other, I will help you when you need me," he said.

So Little Pear and Ergu took care of the two pigs. They put food in one trough, water in the other. Ergu's task was a great deal easier than Little Pear's, for the pigpen was not far from their house. Her mother gave her cooked corn meal and vegetable peelings, all mixed together in a pail; and Ergu dumped this in the food trough, laughing at the pigs, who grunted and snorted and gobbled.

But ay-ah! What a task Little Pear had set for himself! All the water for the village came from a well

out at the edge of the field. The empty pail was easy
to carry, but how heavy the filled one was! By the
time Little Pear had carried it all the way to the pigpen, much of the water had spilled.

"I will help you if you will help me," he said to
Ergu.

"But carrying water is a man's work," Ergu told
him. "Don't you want to be a farmer? Farmers carry
water."

It was true that carrying water was a man's work, √
while preparing food was work for a woman. Little
Pear did not ask his sister to help him again. But sometimes Big Head helped him draw up water from the

well, and sometimes Tang or Yang helped him carry it to the pen. The boys made a game of pulling the well bucket up, up, up, and filling Little Pear's pail. Their clothes got splashed and their shoes got wet, but the pigs got water every day. Little Pear was happy, for he wanted to be a farmer.

One day it rained and everyone was glad, especially the farmers. Rain would soften the frozen fields and melt the ice on the river. The fields could be plowed, seeds could be planted, and soon spring would be here! Little Pear opened the door of his house and looked out at the rain. "Come, Shing-er," he said to his little brother. "Look at the rain."

"Rain," repeated Shing-er. He wanted to run out in the rain, but Little Pear held him back, for the rain would have soaked right through his clothes in a minute.

Ergu, though, was preparing to go out in the rain. She had not forgotten the pigs, whose food for the day was ready. She did not intend to get wet, either, because there was a big umbrella that her father had bought at a fair. The umbrella was rolled up, slim and tall, in a corner of the room, and Ergu brought it forth in triumph and opened it up. When it was open it was as big as a cart wheel! Ergu spun it around, showing it off to her brothers.

"Where did that umbrella come from?" asked Little Pear.

"It came from the Eastern Land," said Ergu, meaning Japan. It was a Japanese umbrella, made of heavy oiled paper, and it was a treasure to be proud of. "Take care of the umbrella and keep dry," said her mother.

Ergu went off in the rain under the big umbrella, carrying the pail of pig food. Little Pear watched her, wishing that he might walk under the umbrella; then his face brightened. It would be his turn next, for he had to go to the well to get water for the pigs, and he must not get wet.

Ergu came back from the pigpen as dry as could be, and Little Pear took the umbrella from her. "It is my turn," he said.

"Umbrellas are not toys," Ergu reminded him.

"I know," replied Little Pear. "But I have to go to the well." He seized the water pail with one hand and balanced the wobbling umbrella over his head. "Wait a minute!" cried Ergu, as he stepped through the gateway. "You don't need to fetch water today, Little Pear."

Little Pear did not hear her, for the rain was pattering on the Japanese umbrella like a lot of little hammers. Raindrops streamed from its rim, but Little Pear kept quite dry. What fun it was to walk to the well under a big umbrella!

But when he came to the well, that was a different matter. Ay-ah! He could not pull up the well bucket without using both hands. He had to set the umbrella on the ground beside him until he had pulled the heavy bucket up and up and up. While he was pulling it up, Little Pear got very wet. Rain soaked through his clothes and poured down the back of his neck. But at last the bucket was resting safely on the edge of the well. Little Pear filled his own pail without spilling too much water and then turned to pick up the umbrella.

The umbrella was not there! Like a cart wheel it had rolled over and over, away across the field. Little Pear dropped the water pail and ran after the umbrella. As he was running he heard his father calling,

"Little Pear!" But Little Pear kept on running, for he did not dare to stop. He thought that his father would scold him for letting go of the umbrella—and the umbrella did not stop. It kept just out of his reach. A wind was blowing the rain away, and blowing the umbrella!

Little Pear ran, and his father ran, and soon his father's long legs caught up with the short legs of Little Pear. Soon Little Pear's father captured the rolling umbrella. "It isn't hurt," said Little Pear.

"No," said his father. "But it nearly rolled back to the Eastern Land, where it came from!"

Little Pear was not scolded for letting go of the umbrella, because after all he was taking care of the pigs. "I told you I would help you when you needed me," said his father.

"And you *did* help me," said Little Pear.

But when they stopped at the house to get dry beside the stove, Ergu said to Little Pear, "I called you, but you didn't hear me. You did not need to carry water to the pigs today. I pulled the water trough out in the rain, and it is filled with water."

And when Little Pear looked, he saw that she was right. The water trough was filled to the brim.

CHAPTER VI

THE SINGING CRICKET

THE toyshop in Shegu was a wonderful place, and children liked to go there even when they had no money to spend. The toyshop man was kindly, and he let the red-cheeked boys and girls look at the toys as much as they pleased, so long as they did not touch them.

One day when Little Pear was minding Shing-er,

he took him to the toyshop. He had no money to spend, but he wanted to look at the toys and he wanted Shing-er to see them too. It was a treat for Shing-er, whose eyes grew round with wonderment as soon as he was lifted over the doorstep of the shop.

The two little brothers were dressed alike in flowered jackets and striped trousers. They looked alike, for Shing-er had a small pigtail that stood up above his forehead, just like Little Pear's. The shopman smiled to see them. "Well, Little Pear," he said, "I see that you have brought your brother to my shop today."

Little Pear bowed politely. "Bow," he whispered to Shing-er.

"Bow," repeated Shing-er, bowing. The shopman was delighted. "You may show your brother all the toys," he said to Little Pear. "But do not touch any of them—unless you have some money."

"I have no money today," said Little Pear sadly.

There were toys on the counters and toys on the shelves. There were dolls for girls, tops for boys, and games for everyone. Little Pear liked the wooden swords, painted with silver and gilt, and he liked the drums made out of gourds, and the bamboo whistles. "Look," he said to Shing-er. "Look, but do not touch."

Shing-er was very good and did not try to touch anything. He looked at the horses made of clay and the tigers made of cloth. He looked at the little round boxes that were meant to keep crickets in; these were favorite toys with Chinese children. "I once had a little box like those," Little Pear told him. "But I lost it before I could find a cricket."

Shing-er murmured, "Cricket," but he didn't pay much attention to the little boxes that his brother was pointing out to him, for he had just spied some pots and pans made of tin. Pots and pans were what Shing-er liked best to play with at home, but he had never seen small toy ones before. He reached his hands

toward a little tin teapot, made like his mother's big one, and he would have touched it if Little Pear had not pulled him away in time. "Don't you remember? You must not touch," Little Pear said sternly.

Shing-er's lip quivered, as though he were going to cry.

The toyshop man stepped over and put his hand on Shing-er's head. Perhaps he thought of his little grandson, just Shing-er's age, or perhaps he remembered how politely the boys had bowed to him. Anyway, he said to Shing-er, "You may have this small teapot," and placed it in his hands!

Shing-er was very happy to have a teapot of his own. It was his favorite plaything for several days, until he decided that he liked his mother's big one better. Then the little teapot was put on a shelf, where it might have been forgotten if Little Pear had not suddenly found a use for it.

One morning Little Pear heard a singing sound, which did not come from the bird's cage. It came from behind the cooking stove, and it was not a cheep, but the special kind of singing sound that only crickets make.

Little Pear searched and hunted until he found the cricket. Here it was, tiny and brown, in the palm of his hand. "Oh, Mother, Mother," he cried, "I have found a cricket at last! Will you give me some money, so I can buy a box to keep it in?"

His mother looked in the cloth bag which she used for a purse, but there were so few pennies in it that she shook her head. "I have to buy flour for bread today," she said to Little Pear. "There must be something here in the house you could put the cricket in."

"I know!" cried Little Pear. "I can put it in Shing-er's teapot."

His mother smiled. That would be just the place for it, she thought; air for the cricket to breathe would come in through the spout. "Shing-er plays with my big teapot, so you can use his," she said, as she lifted

the small one down from the shelf. In went Little
Pear's cricket, safe and sound! "Now I have a new
pet," said Little Pear proudly.

Down the street went Little Pear, to show his cricket
to Big Head. "I never heard of a cricket in a teapot

before," said Big Head. "Crickets belong in boxes, like
the ones in the toyshop."

"I know," replied Little Pear. "But this one likes a
teapot."

Just then the cricket began to sing. "Do you hear it?" said Little Pear.

Big Head nodded. "There are two kinds of cricket," he said. "There are singing crickets and fighting crickets. The fighting ones are best."

"I like the singing ones best," said Little Pear.

The singing cricket lived in the teapot until one day when it somehow escaped—though not because Little Pear kept lifting the lid so often, as Dagu and Ergu claimed. It escaped in the night, when everyone in the family was asleep, and Little Pear was sure that it had squeezed through the teapot's spout.

"The spout is too narrow," said Ergu.

"But the cricket is gone," said Little Pear.

Yes, agreed Ergu, the cricket was certainly gone.

The bird sang, but there was no singing cricket in the house, and Little Pear missed the pet he had had such a short while. He searched everywhere, but

he could not find it. He looked reproachfully at his mother. "You would not let me buy a cricket box," he said. "Crickets belong in boxes."

A few days later Little Pear's mother went shopping by herself and brought home a bright, gay lantern. It was shaped just like a cricket, and it was for Little Pear. "Light the candle inside it, Little Pear," said his mother. "This is a shining cricket."

Little Pear lighted the candle, and the cricket lantern glowed. "This is a new kind of cricket!" cried Little Pear delightedly. There were more than two kinds of crickets, he thought. This was a shining one. Off he went happily, to show it to Big Head.

CHAPTER VII

HOW LITTLE PEAR HELPED
HIS FATHER

IT WAS a fine spring day, kite-flying weather, and many of the village children had gone out to the field to fly their new spring kites. Shing-er had his first kite. He was too little to fly it, but Dagu and Ergu were flying it for him. It was made to look like a giant

78

beetle, red dotted with black, and Shing-er squealed with joy when he saw it rising up into the air.

Little Pear had a new kite too, but he was not flying it. He had more important work to do this morning. His father was plowing a far-off field with the mule to help him, and Little Pear walked behind in the furrow made by the plow. He watched how his father held the plow and guided it. He watched how the plow cut into the earth and turned the brown dirt over.

It was only by watching that Little Pear could learn how to be a farmer. That was what his father told him. Little Pear, though, longed to steer the plow himself. The plow was like a boat, and the field was like a sea. "Will you let me steer?" he asked his father.

"What do you mean?" said his father. "The plow is not a boat, and neither is the mule."

Little Pear trudged behind his father, and for a while he was silent. Then he said, "I know how now. Let me plow!"

His father stopped and wiped his forehead. "It is hard work," he said. "Plowing is for men, not for little boys. Boys can ride mules, though." He picked up Little Pear, and with a swing he lifted him to the mule's high back. "Hold on tight, but don't pull," he added, as Little Pear grasped the rope that was fastened to the mule's harness in place of reins.

Ay-ah! thought Little Pear. How high up he was! From the mule's back he could see the fields in a wide circle around him. The world looked bright and new, and the fields were different colors. This one, just freshly plowed, was brown; another one was green, because spring onions were pushing up their sprouts. Over near the village, where the land was still un-plowed, the dust-colored field was dotted with small figures. Those were the children, flying kites. They were having fun—but not as much fun as he was hav-ing, thought Little Pear. For he was riding the mule! He sat up straight and tall, and clucked encouragingly to the mule as it plodded along. His father followed behind. We are both working now, thought Little Pear. Father is guiding the plow, and I am guiding the mule!

They were two farmers, working. In the onion field another farmer was hoeing between the onion rows. Little Pear's father called to him, "When shall we eat?"

"As soon as you have finished that furrow," the other farmer replied.

Little Pear did not want to stop, but his father was hungry, for he had come out to the field as soon as the sun was up. He had agreed to share a meal with his friend, the neighboring farmer. They had brought bread, and a teapot, and some twigs to make a fire with; all these things were waiting where the two fields met. "You had better go home to your mother," Little Pear's father told him, as he helped him down from his high perch and turned the mule loose. "Your mother will have a hot meal ready for you and the other children, and I am sure you would rather eat dumplings than plain bread and tea."

"What about the mule?" asked Little Pear.

"The mule will stay right where he is," his father said. "When you come back, be sure to bring a pail of water from the well, because the mule is thirsty."

Little Pear hurried. He did not want the mule to stay thirsty, so he decided to bring the water before eating his dinner. "Remember! Take the long way home, and follow the path," called his father.

But Little Pear did not understand why he should follow the path. The short way, straight across the fields, was the road he took. He had forgotten all about an old dry well that was covered over with planks. As

he hurried he watched a kite that was soaring in the
sky. Was that Shing-er's kite, he wondered—the red-
and-black beetle? Yes, Shing-er, Dagu, and Ergu were

still out in the field with several of their friends. Their
eyes were on the kite, and nobody noticed Little Pear.

Little Pear ran, watching the kite. Then suddenly

there was a crash! He had stepped right on a plank covering the dry well, and since the wood had rotted, it crumbled under him! Down he fell inside the well before he could stop himself, and the splintering wood showered over him.

The well had been partly filled with rubbish, so it was not very deep. Little Pear was not hurt, but he was badly frightened. He could not see anything of the world that he had left behind except for a circle of bright blue sky above him. "Help, help! I am in the well!" shouted Little Pear.

Nobody heard Little Pear's cries from inside the well. His father was too far away, and he was busy eating and talking about farming with his friend. Dagu and Ergu and the other children were much closer, but they

were shrieking with excitement over Shing-er's kite. The kite string had got twisted with another child's kite, and everyone was giving advice. "Run this way!" "No, pull that way!" cried the children, and their noise drowned out the sound of Little Pear's voice calling, "Help!"

Little Pear felt the imprisoning walls around him. They were covered with slippery moss, and there was nothing to catch hold of. He felt gingerly for a crack in the bricks where he might wedge his toes, but there were no cracks wide enough to make a stairway for him. Tears rolled down Little Pear's cheeks and

splashed on his jacket. He wondered if he would have to stay in the well all the rest of his life. "Help, help!" he cried again. "I have fallen into the well!"

No human being heard his sad cries, but as Little Pear looked up he saw something blotting out the circle of sky above him. It was not a kite; it was a head with two long ears. Little Pear's face broke into a smile. It was the mule! The mule, at least, had heard him and had not stayed where it was, but had crossed the field in answer to Little Pear's cries for help.

"Go and tell my father where I am," Little Pear said to the mule. But the mule had his own way of rescuing Little Pear. He lifted his head, and brayed and brayed so that everyone could hear!

"Listen to the mule braying," Dagu said to Ergu. "I have never heard him bray so loudly!"

"He is braying beside the old well," Ergu said. "Perhaps he thinks that there is still water in it." The two girls had finally untangled Shing-er's kite string, and they were winding it up and preparing to go home.

The mule kept on braying until Little Pear's father came hurrying across the field. "Where is Little Pear?" he called to Dagu and Ergu. "I sent him home to eat, and to bring back water for this thirsty mule."

"I have not seen Little Pear," said Ergu.

"He is nowhere around," said Dagu.

"Here I am in the well!" cried Little Pear.

Everyone heard him then, for the mule had stopped braying. Little Pear's father, and Dagu, and Ergu, and even little Shing-er ran to look in the well—and there was Little Pear!

It did not take his father long to rescue Little Pear. He tied the mule's rope around his waist and let down one end until it dangled inside the well. There was a big knot at the end, and Little Pear caught hold of it. "Hold tight and don't let go, Little Pear," said his father. And Little Pear did not let go.

When he was out of the well at last, Little Pear felt quite angry. "Why didn't you come when I called?" he cried. "I called and called and called."

"We came as soon as we heard you," said his father, patting his head.

"But the mule came first," said Little Pear.

"The mule called louder, too," said his father.

"He brayed because he had found Little Pear," said Ergu.

Before Little Pear went home to a meal of hot meat dumplings, he fetched a pail of water for the good mule, that had found him. He and the mule and his father had done a lot of work that morning, but it was good kite weather, and Little Pear decided that he would fly his new kite during the afternoon.

CHAPTER VIII

HOW LITTLE PEAR BOUGHT
SOME RABBITS

THE village of Wuku was twice as big as Shegu, and perhaps for that reason it seemed twice as exciting. Instead of one street, there were two streets filled with shops. There was a school, too, and a market place. Every spring a fair was held in the market place of Wuku, and farmers came from far and near to sell their produce. Merchants displayed their wares at the fair. Some had cloth to sell, and others had jewelry, or toys, or artificial flowers.

When his father said that he was going to the fair, there was joy in Little Pear's house, but there was sadness also. The joy was because he was certain to come back with something new. The sadness was because he was going to sell the pigs, which were big and fat now.

Ergu and Little Pear had cared for them such a long time that they seemed like their own. "Don't sell the pigs," begged Little Pear.

"Why not?" said his father. "I bought them so we

could fatten them, and sell them for a good price. Now
is the time to do so, at the fair in Wuku."

To cheer the children up, their father told them that
they might all accompany him to the fair. But Ergu
refused to go. "It will be too sad," she said. She did
not want to see the pigs strapped to the wheelbarrow,
and she did not want to walk near them and listen to
their squealing.

Although Little Pear felt sorry to sell the two pigs,
he decided to go to the fair with his father. The pigs

were going to be sold, whether he went or not; and after all, as he told Ergu, they were going home. They had come from Wuku and they were going back, twice as big and fat as before. "Perhaps the pigs want to go back," he explained earnestly.

"I am not going, though," said Ergu, shaking her head.

So when Little Pear's father wheeled his barrow into the market place, Dagu and Little Pear were the only children with him. Shing-er was too small to travel so far from home; he had been left behind with his mother and Ergu. "Bring me back something, please," Ergu asked at the last minute. "Yes, we will bring you something pretty," promised Dagu.

There were a lot of pretty things in the market place: flowers, and dolls, and singing birds in fancy cages. There were bracelets, earrings, and necklaces to please any little girl; and Dagu wanted to linger over each pretty thing, wondering if Ergu would like it. But Little Pear tugged at her hand, for he heard ducks quacking, and he heard baby chicks cheeping in flat, covered baskets. "Come, let's look at the ducks and chicks. They are pretty too," he said.

"But they are sold to be eaten," said Dagu. "Ergu doesn't want any pets that are meant to be eaten."

The two children were all by themselves in the market place. Their father had wheeled the pigs away to a sort of pen, where there were pigs on one side and sheep on the other. He had told Dagu and Little Pear

to look at all the sights, and to make up their minds what they wanted to buy. "Don't let go of Little Pear, Dagu," he said, fearing that she might lose him in the crowd. And before he disappeared he added, "When

I have sold the pigs I will come and find you and bring you some money."

Dagu kept hold of Little Pear as they threaded their way through the crowd of villagers and farmers, who were buying and selling. The market place was gay with windmills and bright paper lanterns, and different kinds of food set out under tentlike umbrellas. There were cakes and candy, crisp fried fish, and bowls of steamed noodles. There were plates of jellies, and pickled shrimp, and watermelon seeds. No one could look at such good things without being hungry, and Little Pear soon felt very hungry indeed.

He felt in his pocket, which was empty, and looked up at Dagu. "It's time that Father came back with some money," he said.

"Be patient, Little Pear," said Dagu. "He hasn't been gone long. Come away from the food and help

me find something for Ergu." Still holding him firmly by the hand, she led him back to the spot where there were flowers and jewelry and other pretty things.

A kind-faced woman was in charge of a cloth-covered table on which were fans, perfume bottles, and embroidered needlecases. "Do you wish to buy something?" she asked, smiling at Dagu.

"Yes, I wish to buy something for my little sister," said Dagu.

"Is that your sister?" asked the woman, pointing to Little Pear.

Little Pear answered for himself. "No, I am not!" he cried. He didn't want to be taken for anybody's little sister, and he was tired of being taken care of by Dagu. He slipped his hand free, and stood still a moment while Dagu opened out a fan. Then while she was asking the woman the price, Little Pear darted away. He wanted to see if his father had sold the pigs yet.

Off he hurried through the crowd, past the ducks and chicks, and past a cage where some little rabbits were huddled close together. The rabbits looked soft as down, and prettier than kittens. But were they meant to be eaten? Little Pear did not know. He pushed his way past the food tables, where many children were gathered. Then, led by the sound of grunting pigs, he found his way to the pen. He did not see his father, and he could not pick out his own two pigs from the number of large, fat pigs collected in the pen.

He did not look very hard, though, because he had spied a lone gray donkey tied up beside the pen. It had a neat blue saddlecloth and a gay tasseled harness, and Little Pear thought he had never seen anything so pretty.

"Who wants to buy my donkey?" a man's voice was saying.

Before he had time to think, Little Pear said, "I do!"

"Ah," said the man who owned the donkey, "here is a buyer at last." He looked down at Little Pear. "Can you ride it?" he asked.

"Of course," answered Little Pear. "I know how to ride a mule."

"A mule rider, a donkey rider," said the man, and lifted Little Pear to the donkey's back.

Little Pear took the reins in his hands and smiled at the crowd who had come to bargain with the donkey man. But his smile faded when his father came running up to him. "You naughty boy! What are you doing?" cried his father. "I have been looking for you, and Dagu has been looking, and here I find you getting ready to ride off on a donkey."

The donkey man coughed. "The donkey is seven dollars," he said.

Little Pear's father seized Little Pear and set him down on the ground. "Seven dollars is a great deal of money," he said. "It is too much money for a poor man to pay."

"Six dollars," said the donkey man.

"Please!" begged Little Pear.

But his father said, "Six dollars is too much for a donkey. A donkey is not a mule."

"No," agreed the donkey man. "A mule is for work, but a donkey is for riding."

"I want it for riding," said Little Pear.

"Be quiet," said his father. "Where could I find six dollars to pay for a donkey? And where would you keep a donkey if you had one, Little Pear? We must buy food and gifts to take back home with us. You may pick out something; but it must be much smaller than a donkey!"

Little Pear patted the donkey's nose. It was a beautiful donkey, but it cost too much money. His father could not buy it. Still, Little Pear could pick out something smaller for himself. "There are rabbits," he said to his father, and took hold of his hand.

The three miles to Shegu seemed like a long way, and Little Pear was very tired when he reached home that night. He was very happy, though, because he had two rabbits, and they were not to be eaten but to be kept as pets.

As for Dagu, she, too, was tired but happy. She had bought a fan for Ergu that opened and shut, and another one just like it for herself.

CHAPTER IX

MORE RABBITS FOR LITTLE PEAR

LITTLE PEAR's father made a bamboo cage for the rabbits, with a door that slid up and down like the door of the bird cage. While he was working on it, the rabbits scuttled around the courtyard. One was white, one was black, and they were so lively and pretty that Little Pear almost forgot about the gray donkey.

103

He named the rabbits Hei and Pai, the Chinese words for Black and White. But they did not know their names and would not come when he called them. Hei kept hopping toward the gate that led to the

street, and Pai kept jumping over the doorsill into the house. "Watch your rabbits, Little Pear," his father warned him. "A dog could eat one in a minute if it got into the street. And remember, there is a cooking pot in the house!"

Little Pear ran to catch his rabbits. He held them, wriggling, in his arms till his father had finished the cage. When the rabbits were safely popped inside and the door slid into place, Little Pear sighed with relief. "Ay-ah," he said. "Taking care of rabbits is hard work."

"Taking care of anything is hard work," said his father. "How can you be a farmer without working hard?"

"Is farming hard?" asked Little Pear.

"Very hard," said his father.

"But going to school is harder," said Little Pear.

All this time Little Pear had been growing bigger, and there was more and more talk about his going to school. Whenever the talk began, Little Pear turned away; for although he was bigger, he still did not like to think of going to school. "Dagu and Ergu don't go to school," he said to his mother.

"That is because they are girls," his mother said. "I can teach them all that they need to know. But you are a boy, and boys ought to go to school."

Big Head was going to school as soon as the summer was over, and he felt very proud and important. "I am going to study hard, and when I grow up I am going to be a merchant," he said to Little Pear.

"What are you going to sell?" asked Little Pear.

"Toys," replied Big Head promptly.

Little Pear looked at Big Head with new respect. Selling toys would be a very good kind of work, he thought. But selling things meant staying in a shop

all day long, and Little Pear wanted to be outdoors.
"I am going to be a farmer," he said.

"Are you going to school?" asked Big Head.

"Perhaps," said Little Pear.

He thought of the school in Wuku three miles away,
and of the boys who sat in rows, reciting their lessons. Then he thought of the donkey he had seen at
the fair in Wuku. If he had a donkey, Little Pear
thought, he could ride back and forth to school. School
would not seem so hard if he had a donkey to ride!
But how could he buy a donkey? Donkeys cost dol-

lars; and besides, there was no room for one in the small courtyard of Little Pear's home. Little Pear sighed deeply.

"What is the matter?" asked Big Head.

"I wish that I had a donkey, and a stable," said Little Pear.

Big Head thought for a moment. Since he was older than Little Pear, he often had very helpful ideas. "I would like to have a donkey too, so that I could ride to school," he said. "But I would not need a stable for it, because the mule has a stable. If I had a donkey I would keep it there with the mule."

Little Pear looked at Big Head with even greater respect. It was true that the village mule had a nice, big stable, and surely nobody would mind if a donkey shared it.

There was no donkey, though, and there were no dollars to buy one with. Little Pear had to content himself with taking care of his rabbits. Hei and Pai were the only rabbits in the whole village, and all the boys and girls of Shegu liked to come and see them.

They watched while Little Pear fed them cabbage
leaves and carrot tops, and sometimes they brought
food for them from their own homes. "It's my turn,"
one child would say, poking a turnip inside the cage.
"It's mine next," another would say, offering some
lettuce.

One day that summer when Little Pear looked in
the rabbits' cage he had a great surprise. There were
baby rabbits huddled beside the big ones. "Oh, Dagu,
Ergu, come and see!" cried Little Pear excitedly.
"There are a lot of new rabbits in the cage!"

Dagu and Ergu came running, to see for themselves. "Yes, there are four baby rabbits," said Dagu,

counting them. She and Ergu were almost as excited as Little Pear.

The news about the baby rabbits spread through the village, and all the boys and girls hastened to Little Pear's house. "I wish I had a baby rabbit," said one little girl. "So do I!" cried all the other children.

There were many children, though, and only four young rabbits. "There are not enough to go around," Little Pear explained. He decided to keep the little ones with the two big ones, and he told his friends they could come and see them whenever they wished.

The summer was long and hot, but Little Pear did not mind, because he was busy with his rabbits and busy playing outdoors. He saw the green corn sprouting in the fields around the village, and listened to the chorus of frogs in the pond. He never took Shing-er near the pond, but he often went there himself to watch the frogs diving from the bank into the water. Once he was lucky enough to catch one; but when he carried it home, Dagu and Ergu squealed so loudly that he took it back to the pond.

All through the summer the village children came to admire the rabbits and to bring them fresh, crunchy vegetables to eat. The little rabbits grew until they were just as big as Hei and Pai; and no one, not even Little Pear, could tell which one was which. The six big rabbits crowded the cage, and Little Pear felt worried. "Do you think you could build a bigger cage for my rabbits?" he asked his father.

"I can make this old cage bigger with some more bamboo," said his father.

Little Pear's father made the rabbits' cage bigger; but before the summer was over, there was a new surprise for Little Pear and his family! Many more baby rabbits appeared, white, black, and spotted. There were so many that it was hard to count them all.

Dagu said there were eighteen. Ergu said sixteen. Little Pear tried to count them himself, but he had to give up.

"What are you going to do with all these rabbits?" his father asked. "If I make the cage any bigger, it will fill the whole courtyard."

Little Pear looked at his rabbits. There were a lot of them, but there were also a lot of children who wanted to have rabbits. He suddenly had a fine idea. "I could sell them," he said.

"What would you do with your money if you sold them?" asked his father.

"I would buy a donkey," said Little Pear. Donkeys cost dollars, but there were so many rabbits that they could be sold for dollars.

"We have no place for a donkey, Little Pear," said his father.

"There is room in the stable," said Little Pear, remembering what Big Head had told him. "If I had a donkey I could keep it in the stable with the mule."

Little Pear's father was pleased that he had thought of all these things. "I think you will make a very good farmer," he said. "But you must go to school first, like Big Head."

And now Little Pear finally agreed. He must go to school. "Big Head and I can ride to school on the donkey," he said.

All the family gathered around to talk about Little Pear's fine idea of selling his rabbits and buying a donkey. And they all said how nice it would be for Little Pear and Big Head to ride back and forth to the school in Wuku.

"Big Head can look after Little Pear, since he's older," said Dagu.

"And I will look after the donkey," promised Little Pear.

"You will learn so much in school," said his mother, putting her arms around him, "that one day you may become the very best farmer in Shegu!"

CHAPTER X

LITTLE PEAR GOES TO SCHOOL

ONCE more Little Pear's friends came trooping to see the rabbits: Tang and Yang, Big Head and Didi, and all the other children. Great was their joy when Little Pear told them he wanted to sell his rabbits.

"All of them?" asked Big Head.

115

"All," nodded Little Pear. There were far too many rabbits now for one small boy to care for, even if he had not planned to buy a donkey.

"How much will you sell them for?" asked Big Head.

"Thirty cents apiece." That was what Little Pear's father had told him to say.

"That is too much for children to pay," said Big Head, shaking his head.

"Twenty cents," said Little Pear, bargaining like the donkey man.

"Twenty cents!" echoed all the other children. And

so it was settled, though Little Pear's father did not know of the new price until later.

The children clustered around the cage, pointing at the rabbits and saying, "I want that one," or "This one will be mine!" But Ergu said, "The new ones are too little to go yet. You will have to wait awhile, until they grow bigger."

"They grow very fast," added Dagu.

That was true, for soon all the baby rabbits were big enough to be sold. When the news had passed from house to house, the children hurried back. They brought money instead of rabbit food, and they gave Little Pear their money: small silver coins, or copper pennies that could be changed for silver. The pile of money grew and grew, just like the rabbits, till Little Pear thought that he had never seen so much money! In exchange for the silver and copper coins, each child selected a rabbit.

Little Pear's father was in the fields when Little Pear sold his rabbits, but Dagu was there to help him and so was Ergu. They counted money and counted

rabbits until the cage was empty and every smiling
boy and girl had carried a rabbit home.

"Now it is time to go and look for a donkey!" said
Little Pear.

But buying a donkey, he found out, was harder than
selling rabbits. Little Pear had silver coins and copper coins, but not one big, round dollar; he began to

wonder if he had enough money. "Do you think there is enough to buy a donkey?" he asked Dagu. But Dagu did not know, and neither did Ergu.

Little Pear looked at the empty cage, and he suddenly felt sad. All of his rabbits had been sold, and he did not have a donkey.

When his father came home from the fields, Little Pear felt even sadder. His father counted the money himself, shaking his head all the while. "This is not

enough, unless we can find a very small donkey," he said. "Why did you sell your rabbits for only twenty cents apiece, Little Pear?"

"Ay-ah," said Little Pear's mother. "I let Little Pear do that, because he wanted to sell his rabbits to his friends, and thirty cents was too much money for each child to pay."

Little Pear's father agreed. Then he said, "Little Pear is a child, so he should not pay as much for a donkey as a man would pay."

When the pennies and small silver coins had been changed into dollars, there were four silver dollars and they were all Little Pear's. His face brightened when his father said, "We will try to find a small donkey."

The donkey at the fair in Wuku had been sold long ago. But Little Pear went with his father to another, smaller village, and there they met a man with another, smaller donkey to sell. It looked like the little brother of the donkey in Wuku, for it was the same gray color, and it had a saddle, too!

The man asked six dollars for this donkey, but he accepted four when Little Pear's father told him that the money was Little Pear's. "That is enough for a child to pay," he said, as he took the dollars.

What fun it was to ride on a donkey of his own! And how Little Pear enjoyed journeying home with his father! There were rabbits in Shegu, a great many rabbits; but there was just one donkey, and it was Little Pear's. It would carry Little Pear to school and back, and Big Head, too.

Little Pear knew that Big Head would be good company, but he felt rather queer when the morning of his first school day dawned. He wished he had something of his own to take along with him—some small live thing, like a cricket. There were no crickets to be found, but Little Pear remembered the green and yellow frogs that had sung through the summer. He stole out early in the morning and caught a little frog.

When he had slipped it into his pocket he felt much better. Now he was ready to go to school.

The corn was high in the fields around the village of Shegu when Little Pear and Big Head rode gaily off to school. Little Pear held the donkey's reins, Big Head held on to Little Pear, and away they went toward Wuku through the tall green corn.

Their families stood at the edge of the village, waving good-by to them, but Little Pear and Big Head looked straight ahead. From now on they were school-

boys—schoolboys on a donkey—and the world around
them seemed very wide and very exciting.

"There goes Little Pear," said Dagu, lifting up
Shing-er to catch a last view of his brother before he
disappeared. "Little Pear is going to school, for he is
a big boy."

"Little Pear!" called Shing-er.

Little Pear turned and waved. His family caught a
last glimpse of his round, happy face, and the little
pigtail that stood up straight above his forehead.

A moment more, and the donkey with its two riders
had trotted out of sight along the path through the

corn. There would be a long day ahead for Little Pear and Big Head, and a still longer day for their families at home.

"Do you think Little Pear will get into mischief?" asked Ergu anxiously.

"Oh, no," replied Dagu. "He is going to school, and he will be much too busy to get into mischief."

Nobody knew about the frog in Little Pear's pocket, though—nobody except Little Pear himself.

ELEANOR FRANCES LATTIMORE was born in China and lived there until she was sixteen years old. Since then she has made her home in many sections of the United States—New England, the South, and the Midwest—and she now lives in South Carolina with her husband, Robert A. Andrews, and her two sons.

Since 1931, when her first book was published, Miss Lattimore's simple, direct, and warm stories have won thousands of friends among children here and in foreign lands. A gifted artist even before she was a writer, Miss Lattimore illustrates her own stories, and her charming drawings add to their popularity. Many of her books are about American children, but her stories of Chinese children are particular favorites. *Little Pear,* her first book, has already become almost a classic. Readers have long requested more adventures about this heart-warming character, and *Little Pear and the Rabbits,* published twenty-five years later, is the delightful answer.